SNOWMAN WISHES

J.B. HAVENS

CHAPTER 1

Aaron tucked his hands deep into his pockets, shivering as the wind whipped around him and chilled him even further. It was Christmas Eve and he walked alone toward the park in the center of town. Glancing up at the large clock at the entrance to the park pathways, he saw it was fifteen minutes to midnight.

"Almost there. Just a little longer and it will be behind you."

Doing his best to keep his mind from wandering to the Christmas Eve almost ten years ago when his life changed forever was futile. Back before he stopped hanging lights and stockings; the night the magic of Christmas died along with his boyfriend.

The roads were slick with ice and slush that night and they were laughing, singing along with carols on the radio, on their way to Gregory's parent's house. Aaron was looking at the grin on Gregory's face, smiling in return, so in love it was painful, but he hadn't seen the deer until it was too late. When he tried to swerve, the back tires failed to grip on a patch of black ice, and the car fishtailed wildly before flipping.

Turning over and over, rolling down the road. Smashing and crunching as the world exploded around them. Then the night was filled not with joy, but screams and the soul wrecking music of broken glass tinkling onto the pavement. He could still remember the strange juxtaposition of the cheerful Christmas lights reflecting off the shards of glass and a puddle of fluid, slowly leaking and dripping next to his head. It was only later he realized the fluid was blood. He'd never forget the sight of the deer's white tail held high like a flag as it bounded away into the woods, safe and whole.

Shaking loose the memory, he stomped through the snow, hurrying now, desperate to get home to the warmth of his apartment. Physical warmth anyway, it was as bare and cold as this street was.

His boots crunched through the icy layer on top of the snow as he stepped off the sidewalk and took a shortcut through the park. The sound of the breaking ice and snow a fitting counterpart to his feelings. Just on the other side was his apartment building. The lights a beacon, guiding him home. Maybe staying on the shoveled and salted walk would be easier going, but it would be slower. He wanted, no *needed*, this night to be over. He'd put in his cursory appearance with his parents, but now that was done and he could spend the rest of the holiday locked inside, rewatching his favorite horror films.

Not a decoration in sight.

The trees in the center of the park were strung with glittering white lights, the largest pine tree near the gazebo decorated and shining brightly in the darkness. He'd forgotten there was a festival here today. The remnants of the celebration were all around him now. Discarded cups from hot chocolate, candy wrappers, and tinsel. He strode through the debris, head down against the wind, no thoughts in his mind other than reaching his home. Trudging through the snow, single-minded and determined.

Thud

"Ow, fuck!" He stepped back, holding his now throbbing forehead and gaping at what he saw. A life sized, intricately carved ice sculpture of a snowman. If you could call it that. This was no round and jolly Frosty. This was a muscle bound, grinning, and festive snow-MAN. One hand was propped jauntily on his hip while the other hung loosely at his side. He was dressed simply in cut off pants that were held up with suspenders. His mouth was framed by a full beard and stretched in a wide grin with one eye winking. The carving looked so lifelike; he was sure he would come alive at any moment. Handsome and compelling, Aaron couldn't look away from the face. The figure had a blade sharp jawline defined by his well-groomed facial hair and even a dimple in his left cheek, revealed by his bright smile. It should be illegal for an ice carving to be so sexy. Not to mention unfair. Real men, in Aaron's experience, didn't look like this.

"How? What? It's so prefect." A chill raced down his spine and he was reminded of his goal. To leave the merriment behind, hide in his sterile apartment and wait out the holiday. Stepping back, he walked backward, not taking his eyes off the statue. Slow and relucent, he didn't know why he wasn't sprinting in the other direction, but he couldn't seem to tear his eyes from the beautiful statue.

His memory flashed back to when he was a kid, when he still believed in the magic of Christmas. He'd built a snowman with his brother, dressed it with coal for buttons and a carrot nose, topping it with a scarf and old hat. Aaron had spent extra time shaping the face, molding a mouth and eyes carefully in the snow until he had it just right. Then, at the tender age of twelve, he'd looked around to ensure he was alone and pressed his mouth to the snowman. He'd closed his eyes and wished, hoping that it would work. Like the story, that the snowman would come to life and be with him. He'd only recently discovered that he was gay and all things male fascinated him to the point of distraction. Too afraid to tell anyone yet; that simple frigid kiss had been his first real admission to himself that he really *really* did indeed like boys; and only boys.

Nothing had come of it other than a cold and wet mouth, but he'd continued to try anyway. Year after year, snowman after snowman, kissing each. Until he'd met Gregory. Then he'd had someone to kiss him back, rolling in the snow and laughing like children. They'd been so happy and hopelessly in love, he hadn't kissed the snowman that year, it hadn't even crossed his mind to do so; not when he had a real live boy to kiss and hold, warm and safe in his arms.

Until he wasn't.

Now Gregory was just as cold as this snowman and just as unreachable.

Halting his retreat, Aaron stepped forward cautiously, glancing over his shoulder, knowing there was no one around. The clock behind him began to chime midnight. *Dong. Dong. Dong.* He counted them as he stepped closer to the carving.

His heart was aching with emptiness, his soul had shattered the night Gregory died. *Dong. Dong.* Would it hurt to try again? Wish again? Was the magic really gone for him forever? Was this what his life would be like, forever cold and empty? No more laughter, no more joy. Gregory took the light with him when his went out but Aaron, somewhere, deep inside himself; was getting tired of the darkness.

Dong.

"No harm in trying." He muttered aloud, taking the last two steps until he stood in front of the sculpture. "Not snow, but ice is close enough." Resting his gloved hands on the snowman's cheeks, Aaron closed his eyes and made his wish. "Please be real this time. Please come alive. I'm so alone and afraid. I need you this year. Live for me."

Aaron pressed his mouth to the snowman's, gently and softly, a timid first kiss. A tear rolled down his check when he felt nothing but unyielding ice in answer. Pulling back, he blinked away his tears and left a final soft peck on the snowman's lips as he swallowed his sobs. Tucking his face against the hard and frigid shoulder of the sculpture, he wrapped his arms around it in a hug, pretending that arms were holding him back. The last time someone had held him, really held him, was the morning Gregory died. They had woken, cheerful and excited, making love slow and sweet before starting their day. Only to have his love ripped from him that very evening.

A *crack* split the night and Aaron jumped in fear, trying to move back but something held him tight.

"Where are you going, Aaron? Running away already?" A deep voice rumbled from the, now warm, chest under his face.

Warm? How is it warm?!

"What the hell?" Leaning his head back, since his body was held fast, his eyes widened in surprise, for staring back at him was the snowman, only he was no longer cold, no longer icy, no longer inanimate. He was a man. A warm, living breathing, pine and snow scented *man*.

"Not hell. Magic. You've been kissing me and making wishes since you were a boy. The time was never right for me to show you who I am. Now it is." A large warm palm cradled his cheek and his eyes fluttered closed as bliss exploded through him. It felt so good to be touched like this, so intimate and careful. He must have slipped on some ice and knocked himself out and was even now laying prone on the sidewalk, bleeding or something. No way was this real, but he wasn't about to spoil the hallucination for himself.

"My name is Mason."

Aaron blinked at him in shock. "Mason?"

"What? Were you expecting Frosty or something? Oh, my boy, I am not going to melt in the morning, there is no magic hat. You're the magic, you had it all along. You just didn't know it."

"Kiss me again, so I know you're real." Aaron clasped his hands around Mason's neck, his heart hammering in his chest as he tilted his head and leaned forward. Best. Dream. Ever. He hoped he never woke up.

"Glady."

The clock chimed the hour behind them as snow began to fall softly. The wind quieted and somewhere, music played. Aaron's heart felt light and free for the first time in years. Held tightly against Mason's chest, he gave himself over to the feeling blooming in his gut and the electric touch of Mason's lips to his own.

Maybe Christmas miracles weren't just in the movies...

CHAPTER 2

Aaron pulled back and licked his lips, unashamed to be chasing the flavor of Mason still on his mouth.

"I hope I never wake up. If I'm half-dead on the sidewalk, don't tell me. Let me have this."

Laughing, Mason gripped his hips with his huge hands, pulling Aaron closer, aligning their hips. "Does this feel like a dream, Aaron?"

"Yes. Of course, it is. Snowmen carved from ice just don't come alive. This isn't some cheesy Hallmark movie. Magic isn't real."

"I don't know about that, feels pretty real to me."

"Dick jokes from a snowman. Now I know I'm dreaming." Aaron gave into temptation and slid his hands down Mason's chest, his firm pecs filling his palms. "How are you so warm?" Was he this big and hot everywhere? Aaron was dying to find out.

"Would you rather I be cold?" Mason quirked an eyebrow in question.

"No. I like it. I didn't know I was capable of delusions, but it seems I am. The mind is a wonderful thing. If this is what crazy feels like, I'm going to embrace it with open arms."

"Aaron. I'm real. This is real. You're not injured or hallucinating, you're not crazy. How can I prove it to you?"

Tilting his head, Aaron took a moment to think about his answer. "Come back to my apartment with me and if you're still there in the morning, I'll consider it."

Did you just invite a magic snowman back to your place? He had indeed, he thought, as he gripped Mason's hand in his own and towed the big man after him, striding quickly in the direction of his apartment.

Once they reached the doors, Aaron quickly unlocked it and led the way to the elevator. He lived on the fifth, and top floor of his building.

"You aren't a serial killer or something are you?" Aaron looked over his shoulder at Mason while they waited for the elevator. "What am I saying, of course you're not. I wouldn't create a serial killer as part of my delusion."

"No Aaron, I'm not a serial killer. I'm a magical being, there are a lot of us around, you know. We just usually choose not to show ourselves. Humans have a hard time grasping the truth."

"What truth is that?" Aaron asked as the elevator dinged and they stepped in. He pushed the button for his floor, all while checking Mason out in the reflection in the shiny metal elevator walls. The cut off pants were black, in sharp contrast with his pale skin. The red suspenders holding them up were appropriately festive but Aaron's eyes were stuck on the bulge behind the row of buttons in the front. It appeared that Mason was large everywhere. Fitting considering Aaron himself was a bit of a size queen and this was after all, *his* delusion or whatever.

"The truth is the universe and everything in it is far more complicated than most can understand. There are worlds on top of worlds, layered like an onion. Each layer held apart from the one above and below it for the most part, but in a few places they touch. Where they touch sometimes there are rips or holes, allowing beings from other worlds to cross into and out of the others."

"And you're one of those beings, I take it?"

"Yes."

The elevator dinged and the doors slid open. They stepped out with Aaron leading the way to the end of the hall where he lived. He unlocked the door, holding it open for Mason to pass through first. Partly because it was good manners and partly because he wanted to get a peek at what sort of cake Mason was packing.

A full serving, by the looks of it. The soft looking fabric of Mason's pants were tight across his ass, showing each cheek in three dimensional high-definition.

"Stop looking at my ass. Got anything to eat? I've been stuck in my ice form for a few days and I would kill for a burger right about now."

"What now?" Aaron lifted his eyes from the

gloriously full ass of his magic snowman he was currently hallucinating. Was Mason really talking about food right now? His mind was stuck on all the other possibilities of their evening, not food.

"Food? Do you have any?" Mason said again, though didn't wait for Aaron's reply before striding to the kitchen and pulling open the refrigerator door. "Mayo, pickles, lettuce, eggs. This looks promising! Wait, no it doesn't. That's literally all you have in here. Oh wait, here's a piece of cheese." He picked up the bag with the cheese in it, before making a face and tossing it in the direction of the trashcan. "Seriously? What do you live on?"

"Takeout? I don't cook. My mom gives me leftovers sometimes." This was getting weirder by the minute. This delusion wasn't as fun as he thought it was going to be.

Shaking his head, Mason closed the fridge and began to open cupboards, muttering to himself under his breath. All while this was happening, Aaron stood frozen in the doorway, a sinking feeling settling into his gut.

"You okay?" Mason asked, concern evident on his face as he glanced over his shoulder at Aaron. "You look a little pale."

"This…uh…fuck. This is…real? Isn't it? I'm not crazy. You're real!" His heart began to hammer in his chest and his palms grew sweaty. He stumbled back, fear spiking through him along with a shot of adrenaline. "Oh fuck! Who the hell are you!?"

He backed up, freaking out a little more with

every second that went by. What was wrong with him? He'd gleefully led some strange man into his apartment!

"Aaron, calm down."

"Calm down? Fuck you! Get out! I don't know what's happening here, but I don't want any part of it. I'm…I'm not myself. Obviously. This was a mistake."

"Aaron, sweetie, please. Sit down and I will explain everything." Mason advanced on him, both his hands held out to his sides, no doubt attempting to look unthreatening. It wasn't working. Mason, if that was even his name, was huge and–*here–in*–his apartment. It didn't get more threatening than that.

"No. I want you to leave. I don't know what I was thinking, I wasn't, I guess, but you need to go. Right now. I'll call the police." Frantic now, Aaron searched his pockets for his phone, triumph arching through him when he dug it free from his jeans pocket.

Mason snapped his fingers and the phone appeared instantly in his hand. Aaron looked down at his empty palm, his mind struggling to understand what had just happened.

"No police. Just listen, please." Mason put the phone on the breakfast bar behind him, crossing the distance between them, gently cupping Aaron's cheek with his paw sized hand. "No, you're not imagining me. Yes, I am real. Flesh and blood, same as you. I've been trapped here, in your world for about a hundred years."

Aaron swayed, his head going light and fuzzy.

"Nope, nope, stay with me here." Mason gripped

his shoulders, turning him and guiding him down to sit on the couch. "Head between your knees." Gripping the back of his neck, Mason bent him down and holding him there for long moments until Aaron's heart rate slowed and the spots stopped dancing in front of his eyes.

"I'm mostly okay, let me up."

"Sure?"

"No. Not even a fucking tiny bit. But let me up and give me some space."

Mason scooted over to the far side of the couch, putting distance between them even as he angled his body to face Aaron. "That's all you're getting."

"I don't understand."

"I know. Just, breathe a minute and let me explain who and what I am, why I'm here."

Aaron slid both his hands under his thighs while looking straight ahead. Nodding, "Go ahead. I'll um, try."

He felt like he'd stepped into another world, one that looked just like the one where he'd spent his entire life, but now the rules were all backward. He was having a total 'Wonderland' moment and wasn't at all sure if he liked it, but like a bad trip he just needed to get through it. When it was over, everything would go back to normal.

Right?

CHAPTER 3

Mason settled deeper into the couch, allowing himself to sink in and really relax. Well, physically at least. Aaron didn't understand yet, but he'd been frozen and still for days now and the simple act of sitting down was bliss.

"I came into this world about a hundred years ago by accident. I was hiking," seeing Aaron's look of disbelief, he decided to just muscle his way through the explanation and go from there, "Yes, hiking. Anyway, I came over the rise of the hill I had climbed near my home and there was this shimmery sort of light up ahead. Me, being well, me; I walked closer, needing to see what it was. As soon as I was within three feet of the thing it pulled me in. I found out later it was a dimensional tear. I popped out the other side and found myself in a snowy field."

"This is insane."

"I'm aware. Just bear with me here. Anyway, the

rip disappeared and I haven't managed to find another one, well, not one that leads to my home world in any case. So, I've been here." He held up his hands and shrugged. "My magic is different here as well. I can control it for the most part, but sometimes it hiccups and I get stuck in one form for a while. Like the other day. I was stuck as the ice sculpture for three days. Over the centuries, beings from other worlds have inter-bred with humans. Resulting in some humans having some minor magical gifts. Like you do."

"I do?" Aaron's eyebrows shot up toward his hairline and his jaw fell open.

"Yes, which is why I was able to hear you every time you kissed a snowman and made a wish. In most of those cases I wasn't the actual snowman you were kissing, but I heard you all the same. Your intent is what matters. Most I can only hear slightly, sort of muffled. But you're special. I can hear you clear as a bell."

"I…"

"Shh. Just wait." Mason held up his hand, shushing Aaron. "Then you stopped wishing and I stopped hearing you. The last time, do you remember?"

Aaron nodded, quiet now.

"You built the snowman the same as you did every year. Coal buttons and stick arms. Gregory was there with you though. You built it together that year." Mason smiled at the memory. "You were both so happy. You ran your hand down the face of the snowman and patted its cheek, thanked it for being there for you, but you didn't need him anymore."

"I remember. That was you?"

Mason shrugged, "In a sense. Then tonight, it was actually me, not just me hearing you. And... you kissed me." He ran his hands through his hair, then scratching his fingers down his cheeks and through his full beard. "I had to respond. I *had* to. I could hear the pain in your voice and I hadn't heard you in so long. It was a huge risk, showing myself to you. But... you broke through my magic and released me from the ice. That spark you have; it calls to me."

"Now what?" Aaron met his eyes, their blue depths pulling him in, the same way that had for years. The very essence that made Aaron, Aaron, called to Mason's magic and warmed him in a way that he hadn't felt since he was pulled through that rip.

Aaron felt like home.

"Whatever you want. But—I hope you let me stay."

"I need a minute." Aaron rose and hurried down the single hallway toward the back of the apartment and what Mason assumed was the bathroom.

"Well, that could have gone worse, I suppose." Mason said to himself in the now quiet and empty feeling apartment.

CHAPTER 4

Softly clicking the bathroom door closed behind himself, Aaron hurried to the sink and braced his hands against the cold porcelain edge before staring at himself in the mirror.

"What are you doing?" He muttered to himself, not wanting Mason to overhear him talking to himself. Again.

Mason was a being from another world. He had nothing to do with the holidays or winter or any piddly human thing, he was a… refugee? Aaron couldn't believe he was even entertaining the thought of actually *believing* him?

Logic told him that Mason must be a homeless man or something that was suffering from some sort of complex delusion. But even his normally iron-clad logic couldn't explain feeling Mason change from ice to flesh and blood man. And what flesh it was.

Splashing water on his face, Aaron tried to think back to when the last time he'd had sex. He couldn't remember. There had been someone after Gregory, a rebound, nothing more than an attempt to reclaim that part of his life, but it had failed miserably. A bathroom hookup was a terrible idea for getting back on the horse so to speak. He'd crawled into a bottle afterward, clutching Gregorys picture and apologizing. That had been four or five years ago now.

If he allowed himself to suspend belief for a moment, he could admit to himself that he wanted Mason. He wanted the man under him, over him, behind him, on his knees and fuck, sitting on his face. His blood heated along with his face as desire and want barreled through him.

"Give it a night, fuck his brains out, and reassess in the morning?" He'd just be sure to use condoms. Anonymous sex was a thing, he'd just look at it that way. It was a hookup. A one-nighter. He could cheerfully ignore whatever nonsense came out of the big guy's mouth and just instead focus on what he could put *into* said big guys mouth. "Sounds like a fucking plan to me!"

He dried his hands, ran his fingers through his dark hair, it was overlong on the top, but he kept forgetting to go for a cut. No matter, he shrugged, he had a hot guy waiting in the other room. Sure, he was more than a little crazy, but the rumor was that crazy was the best type to fuck anyway. He was going to put that to the test and break his epically long dry spell.

Heading back into the living room, he pushed aside his doubts and allowed himself to be a total guy and just think with his dick. Mason had made it more than clear that he was interested, he would still be sure to confirm, but he hoped they could just get down to business without too much more talking.

"Aaron." Mason stood, looking very unsure and cute at the same time.

"I decided to give it to the morning. I don't know if I believe you, but I'm going to be blunt here a moment, so bear with me."

"Blunt is good. I don't talk to people much, so I'm not very good at it. This is the most speaking I've done all at one-time in years."

Aaron walked closer to him, letting his eyes trail down his bare chest and linger on what was behind the placket of his pants. Then down to his boot clad feet and back up to his face. "I want you and I believe you want me too. For tonight, we're just two people who are hot for one another and who want to spend a few hours getting covered in sweat and cum. Is that something you're interested in?"

"That is one way to put it, yes. But this is more than just one night. You need to understand that." Mason stepped closer then, stopping just in front of Aaron's chest where he could feel the heat coming off the other man. How is he so warm? Shouldn't someone who can take the form of a snowman or ice sculpture be cold?

"I don't know about that. I've decided I'm not thinking about it until tomorrow."

Mason reached up and cradled Aaron's face with both hands, gently, almost reverently. "If that is what you need, okay, but when tomorrow dawns and you see me still here beside you, hopefully still naked and in your bed, you will realize that I have spoken the truth. This may just be one night, true, but what else is equally true; this is just one night of many more to come."

"Shut up and kiss me." Aaron gripped both Mason's hands and leaned in, using his hold to draw the taller man down to him.

Their mouths clashed together, with no hesitation, as if they had been kissing for years already. It was familiar and curled Aaron's toes inside his socks. Heat raced through him, from his mouth down to his cock, and he groaned into Mason's mouth. Licking deep, needing to taste him everywhere. His flavor was all spice and smoke and Aaron could quickly become addicted to it.

Breaking free, he grabbed Mason's hand and towed him down the hallway to his bedroom. He didn't bother with turning on the light, there was plenty from the streetlamp outside. He spun Mason around, shoving him down to sit on the bed.

"I guess we should talk quick first." Aaron began, before yanking his shirt off and flipping open the button on his jeans. "I'm verse, but right now, I need to top. We can switch for round two if you want, but I need to know where you stand."

"I'm…" Mason's eyes were glued to his chest and he swallowed audibly before continuing to speak, "I'm good with whatever. I know I will love it, because it's you that I'm doing it with."

"You're putting a lot of trust into me right now. I

could be an asshole and hurt you." Aaron shoved his jeans and boxers down over his ass, kicking them aside. His chest swelled with pride at the look on Mason's face. It was an expression of pure want and lust. Perfect.

"Ah, hell." Mason reached forward, snagging Aaron's hips with both hands and buried his face into his groin, groaning long and deep. "You smell so good." His voice was muffled and the vibration made Aaron shiver.

His breath left him in the next second, sucked from his lungs, when with no warning at all, Mason lowered his mouth and swallowed Aaron's cock to the root.

"Shit! Mason!" Aaron's head fell back as bliss exploded through every fiber of his being. Mason's mouth was so wet and hot as he began to bob his head up and down, humming with pleasure every so often, Aaron was quickly losing his mind.

His orgasm was barreling up, so fast, so soon, but it had been so long since someone had touched him this way. Mason's tongue joined the party, pushing and flicking against the notch under the head of his dick, then dipping into his slit before starting the torture all over again.

Mason's hand slid up and down his shaft in time with his mouth, squeezing and stroking. Aaron reached down, burying both hands into Mason's hair, wanting to pull and thrust and just savage him, but he held himself in check.

Mason's hands went around to grip his ass as he

pulled Aaron closer, swallowing his cock to the base again. "Oh, fuck me." How he was capable of speech, he wasn't sure. "You're going to make me come."

Pulling off, Mason licked his lips while staring up and meeting Aaron's eyes. "That's the point."

"But I don't want to, yet. I want to be inside you when I blow." Aaron stroked his fingers through Mason's hair, loving the silky texture of the locks against his fingers. "I don't want this to be over too soon. It's been so long…"

"Aaron, I told you, as much as you don't want to admit it, this isn't just one night. Okay? Let me give you this." Mason's expression was open and earnest. Aaron felt a spark flare in his chest, more than lust or burning desire, it was something else. Hope? Refusing to question it further, he nodded his consent.

Wordlessly drawing Mason's mouth to his groin again, Aaron let himself relax into the pleasure and his eyes slide shut as that talented tongue and lips went back to him, sliding and sucking him deep.

He groaned, long and loud, from deep in his chest. Satisfaction burning within him. Mason deep-throated him, again and again, seeming to have no discernable gag reflex. His balls were high and tight and tingles were beginning at the base of his spine, but Aaron didn't fight it this time. He gave into the pleasure and let it surge and wash over him in a rush. He came before he had a chance to warn Mason, but the man didn't seem to mind. He simply moaned in response and Aaron could feel the muscles of his throat swallowing around him, drinking him down and extending his orgasm.

His chest and arms were coated in sweat and his breaths heaved in and out as he panted, trying to regain the ability to speak. His knees wobbled and Mason quickly guided him down onto the bed to lay beside him.

"Are you okay?" Mason asked softly, gently stroking a hand up and down his stomach and chest.

"Ugh."

"No words yet?" Mason chuckled, placing a featherlight kiss right over his heart.

Aaron's eyes grew heavy against his will. He struggled to stay awake but it was as if every bone in his body had been liquified, he was a puddle of jelly.

"Shh. It's okay. Rest now."

Mason's words, the familiar weight of his comforter, and the heavy warmth of a body beside his own were the last things Aaron was aware of before sleep claimed him.

CHAPTER 5

Aaron woke to the sound of a rumbling under his ear.

What the what?

Blinking his eyes open, he found himself staring at his own arm, draped across the enormous chest of a man. *Blink. Blink.*

With a rush, his memories of last night returned to him. Kissing the sculpture, it coming to life and dragging the man, Mason, back to his apartment. The blow job.

Oh, fuck me, the blow job.

He poked a finger into the chest he seemed to be sleeping on, getting an answering grunt in response. He wasn't dreaming after all or having a complex hallucination. This was real, Mason was a real man, being, whatever, and Aaron had brought him home like a lost puppy.

More like a bear, a very gay, master of blow-jobs, bear.

"Go back to sleep." Came a sleepy command from above him. Tipping his head up slightly, Aaron looked up at Mason, whose eyes were still closed and his mouth open slightly.

"Not sure if I can." Why wasn't he freaking out more? Here he was, naked, with a strange man in his bed and he couldn't remember the last time he felt this calm and relaxed. At peace.

"Well, I'm not moving so either go back to sleep or lay there like you are asleep. Your bed is heaven and I don't want to leave it for a good bit."

"You're awfully bossy for someone who is sleeping in *my* bed."

"And you're awfully grumpy for someone who got their dick sucked last night, yet here we are."

Aaron sat up, instantly pissed off. Who the hell did this guy think he was? He scooted away from Mason, being careful to keep the blanket over his groin. "Magic snowman or crazy homeless person, whatever you are and whatever you think this is, it's not over. Get the fuck out."

"You still don't believe me, huh?" Mason asked, casually turning onto his side and propping his head on his hand while staring at Aaron, his eyes shamelessly tracking down every exposed inch of his skin.

"Why should I?"

"Me changing from ice into a man, literally *in your arms* last night wasn't enough?"

"Erm… no." Aaron paused; his thoughts chaotic. Mason was acting like an entitled dickhead and he wanted the man gone, and yet, at the same time he didn't want the strange man to leave. He was so fucked.

"Or how about me knowing that you have a penchant for kissing snowmen and making wishes since you were a little boy?"

"Still no. That could be a lucky guess." Aaron scooted further up on the bed, resting his back against the headboard, putting as much distance between himself and Mason as possible. Mason, who still wasn't leaving.

"How about knowing both your name and the name of your fiancé?"

"You could be a stalker."

"Fine. Fine." Mason stood, throwing his hands up in the air as he muttered to himself. "He wants parlor tricks; we can do that. It's okay, I'm just an over a hundred-year-old magical being from another world, but we'll just Elsa this bitch up."

Aaron gaped, not at Mason's words, or his casual nudity, but at the sight around him. When Mason waved his hands, snow began to fall softly, seemingly from nowhere. He shivered when flakes fell onto his arms and looking down in awe. He couldn't believe his eyes. There were perfect snowflakes on his skin. They shimmered in the light, glittery and cold. He looked around him, snow was piling up on the covers, gathering in the creases and folds of the blanket. He gathered some on his fingers, touching it to his tongue. Puffing out a breath, it fogged in the air in front of him. The room was now as crisp and frigid as a winter day outside.

His eyes widened, "This is real."

"Yes, Aaron, it's real. In my own world, I had the power to create huge storms of ice and snow. Here though, my magic is weaker and this is about all I can manage. That and changing forms. Which doesn't always work out, since I get stuck on occasion, as you saw last night."

He wasn't stuck in some fucked up waking dream. Mason had magic, for lack of a better term. Though magic did fit, what else would you call the ability to make it snow indoors?

A realization struck Aaron then, that not only was Mason the only one of his kind here, but he was weakened and not himself. He was see-sawing emotionally between disbelief, surprise, and heartbreak for Mason. He's been all alone, for over a hundred years. Aaron himself had been alone for ten and he was clinging to sanity by his fingernails, he had no idea how Mason had lasted so long.

"Why me? Why now? I'm sure I'm not the first person you've met that you liked or whatever."

"Course not."

Mason waved his hand again and the snow stopped. Aaron was full on shivering now, a layer of snow coating his bed, which also disappeared with another casual wave of Mason's hand. Thankfully, since the last thing he wanted to deal with was wet bedding.

"It took me a while to even consider interacting

with humans, but what choice did I have? I came to terms with being stranded here and decided to make the best of it."

"What now?" Aaron climbed from bed, searching for his discarded boxers. He felt vulnerable and off kilter, being naked wasn't helping.

"Breakfast. I don't know about you, but I'm starving." Mason paused long enough to tug his pants up over his delectable ass before leaving the bedroom. Aaron groaned mentally, his thoughts quickly getting stuck on the image of diving between those meaty cheeks face first. Moments later, while Aaron was still standing frozen, he heard pans clanging around and the sound of running water.

He pulled on a t-shirt and some pajama pants before quickly brushing his teeth and splashing water on his face. He needed just that little bit of care to feel more centered. In less than twenty-four hours he felt like his entire life had been turned on its head.

Staring at himself in the bathroom mirror, he tried to see the change he felt, yet he looked the same as ever. Maybe a little better even, the perpetual dark circles under his eyes were a little lighter. He'd slept better last night than he had in years. He wasn't sure if it was the steller blowjob, the comfort of sleeping next to another person, or a combination thereof.

"Food first, then you can revisit your existential crisis."

Making his way to the kitchen, he was greeted by the sight of Mason stirring something in a pan on the stove and swinging his hips to a tune he was humming. The material of his pants pulled tight on his hips as they swayed, highlighting the firm muscle beneath. He was unabashedly an ass man and Mason was packing a serious specimen of glorious gluteus maximus.

"I used the four eggs you had. I hope it's enough for us both. Of course, everything is closed today so we can't even run to the store."

"Yeah, erm, sure. That's fine. Use whatever you want."

Mason looked at him over his shoulder, winking before saying "If I'm still hungry, I could always have another protein shot."

Aaron gaped, his mouth falling open. This man was nothing but constant surprises. "You just made a dick joke."

"Sure did. But it was no joke. Last night was fun and I'd love a repeat. Though call me greedy, but I'd like a little something-something for myself. I slept all night with my cock as hard as fence post."

Blushing, Aaron looked at his bare toes. He was embarrassed he'd passed out like a total douche and hadn't reciprocated. "I'd like that. I mean, I don't know whats happening here and I still have about two million questions, but last night was amazing. It's… well…it's never been like that for me. That…intense, I mean."

Mason arched a brow before taking the pan off the heat. "Even with Gregory?" He opened and closed cupboards, no doubt looking for plates. Aaron brushed past him, pulling two plates from the cabinet next to the stove.

"Gregory was so long ago, it's hard to remember, if I'm completely honest. There were a few times that really stick in my head, our first time of course and a few others. But… I don't know." Aaron trailed off, not able to find the words to express what he was feeling right then.

"Aaron, it's okay. I think I understand what you're saying."

"And can I just say that it's totally fucking weird that you know about him? About us?"

Mason shrugged, plating the eggs and carrying their breakfast to the dinette table. He rarely had company over, in fact, he didn't have any friends to invite over anyway. Other than his mom occasionally coming over for a cup of coffee, so he hadn't seen the need for a bigger table.

"Yeah, I can see how that's weird for you. But I can't pretend that I don't know. And also, it's not as if I know everything. I'm not omniscient. I only know what I've personally seen."

"That makes me feel a little better." Sitting down across from Mason, he surveyed his plate. Two slices of buttered toast rested next to two fried eggs. "This looks delicious."

Pointing at him with his fork, Mason admonished, "Yeah, but we're officially out of food so we'll need to come up with a plan for lunch."

"We?"

"Yes, we. I told you, this wasn't going to just be

one night. When you know, you know, and Aaron—*I know.*"

"You realize that makes zero sense, right?" Aaron tucked into his food, using the toast to mop up the runny yolk as it ran across his plate. He was starving and hadn't even realized it until he began eating. "Oh, and another thing." He began, pausing to swallow before continuing, not meaning to talk with his mouth full, "Where do you live? Why can't we go eat your food?"

"Sure, I guess we could go there. I like it better here though." Mason retreated to the kitchen, coming back carrying two cups of coffee, handing one to Aaron before sitting back down.

"Why?"

"It's warmer."

"Huh? Do you live in a cave or something?"

Laughing, Mason snorted into his coffee cup. "No. I don't live in a cave. But it's hard to get a mainstream job and have enough income for a nice place when you don't have any documents." Quirking an eyebrow, Mason wiped his mouth and gathered his now empty plate.

"I didn't think of that. So, what do you do for income?"

"I rob old ladies."

Aaron glared, not believing him for a second.

"Okay, fine. I don't rob old ladies. I take odd jobs where I can find them and save my money for when there isn't much work. I don't mind the weather so I do a lot of shoveling and stuff in the winter. The people I work for are always so amazed at how quickly I can clear the snow." Mason chuckled, holding his hand out flat and wiggling his fingers. A perfectly formed snowball appeared above his hand and then disappeared a second later.

Aaron chuckled, surprising himself at how quickly he was getting used to the reality that this man was literally magical.

CHAPTER 6

fter breakfast and a quick clean-up for them both in the shower, separately, much to Mason's disappointment, they headed out for a walk. Mason led the way to his small apartment, needing to get some different clothes in any case. He was still dressed in the odd-looking pants and suspenders. Maybe he wasn't human in the same sense that Aaron was, but he'd lived here long enough that he'd gone native, so to speak. On his world, men didn't bother with shirts, but typically it was noticed here when a man walked around bare chested all the time. Though in these more modern times it was less commented on. Fifty years ago, on the other hand, was a different story.

As if Aaron could read his thoughts, he asked, "I bet you've seen a lot, huh? The history alone that you must have witnessed is mind-boggling. The industrial revolution, the Great Depression, the World Wars, and that's just the things that come to mind right now. I'm sure there is tons more that I can't even imagine."

Chuckling, Mason took Aaron's hand, twining their fingers together. "Sure. Take this for instance." He held their hands up. "Even just forty or fifty years ago, we wouldn't have been able to do this. I was in New York for the Stonewall. It was a moment where I was proud to be among the humans and seeing them standing for what is right."

"That's just…I can't wrap my head around it. Talk about an age gap."

Laughing, Mason stopped and pulled Aaron close, kissing him quickly. "Don't worry about it too much, I'm young in heart and body."

"So, you really can't go home?" Aaron asked, stepping back and reclasping Mason's hand. He liked holding Aaron's hand, maybe it was juvenile of him, but it sent a tingle up his arm just the same.

"I really can't."

"Isn't there some way to reopen the…whatever it is you came through?"

"The rift? No." The thought didn't make him as sad as it used to. He'd found so many things here to love that even if he could go home, he wasn't sure if he would. He met Aaron's eyes, warmth building in his chest.

"Are you familiar with the multiverse theory?"

"Sort of." Aaron's brow wrinkled as he thought, a gesture that Mason found adorable.

"Basically, the universe is massive and full of different worlds. Each world is a different version of this one. Some don't have humans at all. There is even one where the asteroid never hit and dinosaurs still rule. Following me?"

"Yeah."

"So, my world is just one version of this one, where people are born with magic. The worlds connect in places. Like a piece of paper folded in half. The two halves exist independent of each other, but touch in places. My world and this one had a tiny tear open and that's how I slipped through, but it's closed now. I can alter the moisture in the atmosphere and make it snow, but I can't change the fabric of the universe. It doesn't work that way. Unlike in pop-culture and fantasy novels, there is no magic spell to change the cosmos."

"That sucks, I'm so sorry."

"I've had a long time to come to terms with it, please don't be sorry on my behalf. It led me here, to you, so I'm okay with it."

Aaron's eyebrows shot up, but he didn't say anything, just turned forward and continued walking at his side.

"Enough about me, I know what your cum tastes like but I don't know what you do for a living."

Aaron made a choking sound and whipped his head around to glare at Mason. "Say it a little louder why don't you? Fuck man."

"What? You're not embarrassed, are you?"

"Of course not! But I also don't go around announcing that I got a blow job either."

"Well, you should. I had nearly as much fun as you did."

"Anyway!" Aaron rolled his eyes, "I work from home mostly, as a virtual assistant to different companies. I handle their social media posts, stuff like that."

"And you find that fulfilling?"

Aaron shrugged. "Not really, but it pays the bills and gives me a lot of freedom. Most people can't say the same."

"You should be doing what you love, not just what is practical."

"Work is a means to an end. A fact most adults learn to accept."

Mason stopped in front of his apartment door, reluctantly letting go of Aaron's hand to unlock it. He lived in a small one-bedroom apartment above a laundry mat. The benefits of which is that it's quiet at night and his home always smelled like fabric softener. He was easy to please, what could he say? Leading the way up the steep and narrow staircase, Mason tried to think if he'd cleaned up before leaving the last time or not. He wasn't overly worried about it, but the last thing he wanted was Aaron to walk into his home and think he lived like an animal or something.

Hesitating at the door, keys in hand, he looked over his shoulder at Aaron, "How harshly will you judge me if my place is a mess?"

"Not at all. But I will judge you if you don't let me

in there soon. You may not feel the cold too much, but I'm freezing my balls off."

"We can't have that. I quite like your balls."

Aaron snorted in laughter as Mason opened the door. He braced himself, but everything seemed fine as he stepped inside. No heavy smell of rotting food or garbage, just a faint hint of stale air.

"It isn't much, but I don't need much." He stepped aside, letting Aaron walk past him before closing and locking the door behind them. Mason looked around his home with new eyes. It was little more than an efficiency apartment, with a small kitchenette and no table. He had a loveseat and a coffee table where he ate his meals and an old, but functional TV. Down a hallway that was so short it could hardly be called that, was his bedroom on the left and his bathroom directly across on the right. That was it. Three rooms.

"Mason, seriously, it's fine." Aaron turned to him, taking both Mason's hands into his own. "I know we don't know each other very well, but do you really think I'm the type of person to judge someone for the size of their apartment?" Aaron's expression was earnest and open. How was this happening? In all his years in his world and this one, he never thought he'd find someone for him. But he knew, deep in his gut, Aaron was that person. His other half, the missing piece of his soul. There was so much he wanted to learn about this sad human and he intended to spend the rest of his life doing just that.

"I guess not." Mason's pulse was thrumming,

pounding at the realization that his future was standing before him.

"Are you okay?" Aaron tilted his head to the side, squeezing Mason's fingers.

"Y-yeah. I'm good. You?"

"Dude, you're acting weird. Which is saying something."

Chuckling, Mason tugged Aaron closer, pressing their chests together, and wrapping his arms around the small of Aaron's back. He wanted to get him even closer, skin to skin. He wanted Aaron's breath on his neck, his taste on his tongue, his moans and cries of pleasure filling his ears.

"You make me feel things I never thought I would."

Aaron's eyes widened and his breath came faster. "What kind of things?"

"Important things."

"This is a heavy conversation considering we only just met last night."

"Time has no meaning; time is a construct developed by humans and beings like myself to bring order to an otherwise chaotic world. Nor does time have weight."

"You aren't going to be happy until you have me in a full-on existential crisis, are you?"

Laughter exploded from Mason, his chest aching with the force of it. "I've been happier in the past twelve or so hours than I have been in the last five decades." Mason didn't give Aaron a chance to respond, instead, he ducked his head and captured his tempting mouth. The taste of his human exploded through him, a groan rumbling free even as he tugged Aaron tighter against his still bare chest. The heat from his skin permeated into him, warming Mason's very soul.

"I can relate. This feels so surreal. Out of this world and impossible. Like I'm trapped in a dime store romance novel."

"Does this feel impossible to you?" Gripping Aaron's hand, Mason led it to his hard length. "I'm aching for you."

Aaron swallowed audibly, his fingers tightening around Mason's rigid cock. "Even if this is a dream, I don't ever want to wake up."

Grinning, Mason thrust his hips against Aaron's hand. "You're not dreaming." Fisting Aaron's hair at his nape, Mason hauled him closer and sealed their mouths together. Aaron's flavor exploded through him, like mulled wine, he couldn't get enough. He was past want and barreling unstopping right to need. "You taste so good."

"Umm..." Aaron hummed, his hands gripping Mason's sides, digging into the flesh, keeping their bodies pressed tight together. "So do you." Smirking, Aaron pulled back, running his palms up and down Mason's chest, lightly tugging on his chest hair. "I love how big you are."

Grinning wolfishly, Mason palmed Aaron's ass, "We'll see if you're still saying that when I'm buried inside you." He shuffled them backward, aiming for his bedroom. Was this going fast? Yes, yes it was. Did he care? Not a fuckin' bit.

"Who says I'm going to bottom? You didn't even ask." Aaron grinned, nipping at Mason's chin before licking along the seam of his lips. Moaning, Mason stopped walking and cradled Aaron's face in both palms, deepening the kiss until their teeth were clacking and he was sure he was about to blow in his pants at any moment. Retreating, gasping and trembling, Aaron smirked up at him. "Rude."

"I don't care if you're under me, above me, or behind me. It's not a matter of who's dick is where. I need you. It's that simple. If you want to top. Fine. If you want to switch. Also fine. Just as long as your skin is against mine and your cries of pleasure are in my ears."

His hands shaking, Aaron glanced over his shoulder at the bedroom door before taking Mason by the hand and tugging him along. "That works for me."

CHAPTER 7

Aaron's heart banged in his chest, thumping and racing, matching the breaths that gasped from his lips. He'd never been this needful, this desperate to be with another person. Even with Gregory. Which was a thought he didn't want to examine too closely. Not now. Not when Mason was staring down at him, when the sexual tension between them was so thick, he was surprised he couldn't see it hovering in the air between them.

"Aaron…" Mason began, but Aaron cut him off with a quick kiss. He pulled his shirt off, dropping it to the floor. Sliding his arms around Mason's thick waist, moaning at how good his skin felt, Aaron pressed their bare chests together. A groan rumbled from Mason's throat as he returned the embrace.

"I love your skin against mine. You're so soft and warm."

Smiling wryly, Aaron rubbed his throbbing length against Mason's hip, "Not too soft, I hope?"

Growling Mason clutched Aaron under his ass cheeks and picked him up, an undignified squeak escaping Aaron. Wrapping his legs around Mason's waist and his arms around his neck, he was raised slightly above his lover's head. Looking down at him was different, but the clear blue of Mason's eyes glimmered, his desire plain.

"Not too soft at all." Mason took his mouth again in a scorching kiss. Kneeling on his bed, Mason cradled the back of Aaron's head, laying them down and sinking his weight against him.

Aaron gasped, surprised how much he loved the press of the other man's body pushing him into the mattress. He was surrounded, encompassed, and cradled. "God…" He gasped, thrusting his hips up helplessly, need riding him hard. He needed more. More friction, more skin, more everything. "Please."

"Shh, I've got you." Retreating slightly, Mason quickly dropped his pants, kicking them aside before tugging Aaron's free. Naked and exposed, Aaron didn't feel even a sliver of embarrassment, only desperation. Spreading his legs shamelessly, he tugged Mason back down on top of him.

They groaned simultaneously as their cocks aligned and rubbed together. Jerking without thought, just reacting, Aaron thrust their lengths together. Pre-cum oozed from them both, slicking the way.

"Aaron. Fuck." Mason tucked his face into his neck, licking a stripe up and to his ear, where he sucked his earlobe into his mouth. Shivers broke out all along Aaron's shoulders and arms and he shuddered helplessly.

"I know. God, it's so…" Words failed him as Mason reached down, his huge hand pressing their cocks together, giving them both firm, slow pulls. The velvet heat of Mason against his own painful erection was almost too much. "Stop. I can't. I'll come. Mason!" Aaron's hips twitched and his toes curled before Mason took pity on him and removed his hand. Sweat beaded on his brow and he couldn't catch his breath. This feeling was intense, so much more than just desire. It far surpassed that, overwhelming him to his core.

"Baby, breathe." Mason chuckled, kissing his way down his chest. Stopping to scrape his teeth over his nipple, earning another throaty moan from Aaron. "Humm, your nipples are sensitive. We'll revisit that." He licked and nibbled a path down his chest and stomach, until his cock was bumping and nudging against Mason's chin. But he ignored it, moving lower to suck at his balls. Pulling first one, then the other into his mouth.

"Oh fuck." Aaron cried out, his hands going to Mason's hair. He let his legs fall open further, plating his heels into the mattress. He wasn't sure if he was wanted to pull Mason closer or push him away, his emotions were rioting, his heart beating a tattoo against his ribs as moans and cries of pleasure ripped from his throat. His legs were shaking, his toes curling. Mason's large hand circled his cock, tugging and twisting up, circling the head as his mouth went from his balls to his taint, to the ultra-sensitive skin where his thigh joined his groin. Mason's beard tickled him, forcing him to break out in goosebumps. How could the scrape of Mason's beard be so erotic?

"You're a trembling mess. I love it." Mason spoke against his sack, the vibration making Aaron twitch and moan like a whore. Mason palmed the backs of Aaron's thighs, pushing them up toward his chest, exposing his hole to his gaze. "Hum. Lookie there. Fuck, you're gorgeous here. Have I mentioned that I'm an ass man?" Winking up at Aaron, Mason lowered his head and licked a path from Aaron's tailbone to his balls.

Aaron jerked, shoving his ass harder against Mason's face, who chuckled in response before reaching down and spreading him apart with both hands and diving back in face first.

"Oh fuck... me... shit... god dammit... Mason!" Aaron babbled as Mason ate him. He'd had rim jobs before, but he'd never felt anything like this before. When Mason's tongue breeched him, Aaron's hips flew up and he squealed, a sound he'd never made before in his life but he couldn't help it. His dick was so hard it hurt and he was leaking all over his belly. Mason hummed and just as he was sure he was about to come from Mason's tongue alone, freezing cold air blew across his hole, making him shriek.

"God!" The contrast of cold air and the heat of Mason's mouth nearly sent him over the edge. Again.

"Magic can be fun." Mason's eye twinkled up at him from between his legs.

"If you don't fuck me right now, I swear to god I'll kill you."

Grinning, Mason scooted up, his lower jaw shiny which he wiped on his bicep before reaching over to the bedside table. He jerked open the drawer so hard it fell out and onto the floor with a crash.

"Dammit."

Laughing, Aaron covered his face with both hands. His legs were still twitching like live wires from the rim job from heaven. Or was it hell? Aaron wasn't sure. All he knew was that he needed Mason's dick fucking him into the mattress or he was sure he was going to go up in flames and die. Death by edging, it's a thing. Somewhere. It had to be.

"Yes! Got it!" Mason shouted in triumph, holding up a bottle of lube. Glancing down, Aaron took in the sight of Mason's cock. It was… intimidating, to say the least. Long, thick, and shiny with pre-cum, he swallowed, suddenly nervous. He hadn't bottomed in a long time, let alone had something that big shoved up his ass.

"If it's too much, you can top." Mason said softly. Rubbing his palm up and down Aaron's chest.

"No. It's just been a long time and you're not exactly little. Let me up, it'll be easier for me to take you if I'm on my hands and knees."

"I want to see you."

"I want to see you too, but to start, I think this will be easier. I'll have a little more control."

Nodding, Mason moved back enough so Aaron

could flip over. He rose up on his hands and knees, spreading his legs apart and tilting his hips.

"Fuck." Mason ran his hands down Aaron's back and over his ass cheeks. "I like this. You're so fucking beautiful."

"Enough sweet talk, get me ready."

"So, bossy." Mason chuckled, but the snap of the lube cap opening followed. Mason squeezed the cold gel onto his hole, spreading it around with his thumb. He'd already softened somewhat from Mason's tongue. Mason breached him with one finger, sliding it deep past his knuckle in one go.

"Ugh, fuck." Aaron lowered to his elbows, resting his forehead on the backs of his hands, panting as Mason added a second finger. Working them in and out, adding more lube, and scissoring his fingers. "That feels so good."

"Just wait until I'm inside you."

Two fingers became three, the burn intense but fleeting as pleasure overtook him. The pain faded and merged, Mason thrusting his fingers in and out until Aaron was moaning and pushing back, taking all his fingers easily. The squelch of lube was almost obscene, but it just turned him on more.

"Mason, please, I'm ready."

Aaron heard Mason lubing up his cock and a moment later the broad head was pushing against his hole. "Deep breath and push back." Mason pushed forward firmly as Aaron met him, bearing down and pushing back against him. The head of Mason's dick popped past the first ring of muscle, pain flaring through Aaron and tensing his muscles.

"Breath baby. Push back when you're ready." Mason had one hand gripping his hip and the other painted a soothing path up and down his back, relaxing him. "That's it." Mason slipped a little deeper, pulling back a little and then thrusting forward, working himself in and out slowly, going deeper with each jerk of his hips. "Fuck you feel so good. Shit, I'm not going to last long. You're so tight…" Mason's words trailed off on a grunt.

Aaron panted, focusing all his attention on his hole, the stretch and burn, the incredible fullness. It hurt, yes, but the pain was morphing into pleasure as his muscles continued to ease, stretching to accommodate Mason. A little deeper and the head of Mason's cock pegged his prostate directly, a cry exploding from his mouth and a shiver wracked his body, making Mason sink even further inside him.

Surely, he was all the way in? Right? Fuck!

"That's it. Almost there." Mason surged and retreated, grunting, his hands squeezing Aaron's hips so tight he knew he'd have bruises. The thought just spiked his desire higher. Finally, Mason's hips met his. "Aaron, God, you did it. That's all of me. I'm inside you."

Gasping, Aaron's arms trembled, "Yeah, I'm aware."

Laughing, Mason pulled back slightly before thrusting forward, hard.

"Ugh. Do that again." His erection had softened at

first but he was hard as stone again. Rocking back, Aaron began to fuck himself on Mason's thick cock. He'd always thought of himself as a size queen, and Mason was proving him right. His ass was stretched so wide, he was so full, near to bursting. "So good. Don't stop."

Growling, Mason pulled him back by his hips, countering his thrusts in. Their skin was slapping together, a chorus adding to the sounds being driven from their throats. Mason was loud, matching Aaron as he relaxed even further. The pain was gone completely now, only pleasure remained. Ecstasy sparking through his whole body, Mason hitting his prostate with every thrust.

He didn't have the strength to lower a hand and jerk himself, for the first time in his life, sure that he didn't need to. He was going to cum untouched. The orgasm built along the base of his spine, drawing his balls up tight against the base of his dick.

"Mason. Oh fuck. Oh God. Yes! Don't stop. Just like that…" He words failed, his breaths sawing in and out as he struggled for air.

"You're going to cum for me." Mason reached up, taking a fist full of Aaron's hair, pulling his head up. "I'm fucking the cum right out of you, aren't I?"

"Yes. Fuck. Fuck. Ugh." Incoherent sounds fell from his lips.

"Now!" Mason roared, his dick jerking inside him as he began to come. Mason's cock flooded his insides with heat, the feel of it sending him over the edge. Aaron's orgasm exploded out of him, his cock spurting cum and his ass clamping down on Mason. He shoved himself back, fucking himself over and over as his orgasm went on. White lights danced behind his eyes and something close to screams filled the air around them.

Shaking and gasping, he collapsed forward, all his strength left him, his limbs were jelly. He kept twitching, aftershocks shooting through him, making him groan. Mason had followed him down, still buried inside him, thrusting gently and moaning as Aaron reflexively tightened around him.

They both laid there for long moments, catching their breath, sweat cooling on their skin.

"I'm so sensitive, I'm almost afraid for you to pull out."

"Same. But it has to be done. Ready?"

"No."

But Mason had already started to move before Aaron spoke, they both groaned. Wetness leaked out of Aaron, running down the crack of his ass, coating his balls, mixing with lube. Along with his own wet spot he was laying in, Aaron was uncomfortable to say the least. He'd get up and clean himself up in a minute. Or two. Once he legs started working again.

"I'm over a hundred years old. I've had more partners than I can count. But that was the best sex I've ever had. When can we do it again?"

Laughing, Aaron turned his head to look at Mason, a sweaty length of hair falling across his forehead. "Give me twenty minutes. But it's your turn to bottom. My ass can't take that monster cock again so soon." Already soreness was blooming, but it was a pleasant sort of pain, one born of a good time. Not a 'I'm hurt' sort of pain, instead one he would treasure, remembering what had caused it.

Grinning, Mason leaned forward, kissing him deeply. "Deal."

CHAPTER 8

Christmas day passed for them in a haze of sweaty skin as they glutted on each other. That had been three days ago. Aaron was back at his apartment and sitting at his computer, zoning out–yet again–when he was supposed to be working.

His thoughts kept returning to Mason, to the sex, yes; but also, the laughter they'd shared. He hadn't felt that light and free in longer than he could remember. It was as if a weight was lifted from his shoulders while he was with the magical being. He hadn't thought of Gregory much in those sparse few hours with the other man. Guilt surfaced. Followed by anger, at himself mostly. Wasn't ten years enough time to mourn? Gregory was gone and a part of Aaron would always love him, but Aaron was still alive. Did he really want to spend the rest of his life living as a shell? Sad and despondent, never feeling joy again?

No. No he didn't.

Picking up his phone, he scrolled to Mason's contact. Opening a text, he thumbed out a message:

'Hey'

Mason's response came moments later, 'Hey yourself.'

'What are you up to today?'

'Nothing much. No work until it snows again.'

Aaron bit his lip, thinking of what he wanted to say. Well, he *knew* what he wanted to say but he wasn't ready to go there yet. *I miss you. Come over. Do you feel this connection too? Three days feels like three weeks.*

'Stop thinking so much, I can practically hear it from here. Relax, Aaron.'

'Shut up.'

'You're the one who texted me?'

Rolling his eyes, Aaron spun around in his office chair. Twice.

'If you could have any super power, what would it be?'

'Aaron. Did you forget I'm literally a magical being? I can make it snow. I HAVE superpowers already…'

"Fuck." Aaron said out loud to himself, his face heating. "Duh, you idiot."

'Same question to you.' Mason asked, adding a winking emoji to the end of the text.

Aaron didn't even hesitate, knowing the answer already.

'I'd want to fly so I can do the cool superhero landing like Thor.'

'Haha. I love that. I'd offer to take you flying, but sadly, that is not one of my superpowers.'

They both fell silent for a few minutes, the smile frozen on Aaron's face. What was this? Huffing, he decided he didn't care. He wasn't going to waste time asking questions as a guise to cover up what he really wanted to know.

'Is it weird for me to tell you that I miss you?'

'Not at all. I miss you too. I can come over, just say the word.'

Not giving himself even a moment to consider his actions, he went with his heart and his gut. There was nothing wrong with grasping the happiness he'd found so suddenly with both hands.

'Word.'

Putting his phone aside, he shut down his computer, promising himself he'd finish work later. Glancing down at himself, he saw he was still in his lounge clothes and he hadn't showered. "Shit."

Rushing through to his bathroom, he stripped in record time and took the world's fastest shower. He brushed his teeth quickly and dressed in his favorite pair of broken in jeans and a soft t-shirt. Forgoing boxers and socks both, he ran his hands through his hair, huffing when it didn't lay the way he wanted. "Whatever, it doesn't matter. Stupid hair anyway."

Making his way out to the living room, he double checked that he hadn't left dirty underwear laying around or something equally embarrassing. He normally didn't care, even a little bit, but for some reason he wanted Mason to feel welcome and at home. *Some reason*, right. He knew exactly why he was feeling the way he did. He wanted the man, being, male, whatever, to love being here, to always want to be in his apartment with him.

"Shut up, you sound like a fucking Hallmark movie you loser."

A knock sounded on the door, breaking into his not-quite-so internal monologue. Striding with what he hoped was real confidence to the door, he turned the knob and opened it. Standing there, with one hand braced on the doorjamb was Mason. He was just as massive as Aaron remembered, his hole twitching in memory.

"Hi." Mason said, grinning with what could only be described as a wolfish grin. Aaron suddenly felt a lot like prey about to be devoured.

Yes, please, eat me. All of me.

"Well, that's direct. But you'll have to let me inside for that. I don't imagine you want your neighbors to see me face first between your ass cheeks out here in the hallway?"

Aaron's face heated so fast he went lightheaded for a moment. "Did, I, ugh, say that out load?"

"Sure did, dumpling." Planting a hand on Aaron's chest, Mason pushed gently, but insistently, "Come on. In you go."

"Dumpling?" Aaron raised an eyebrow in question.

"Yeah, because you're delicious."

"Fucking hell." Rubbing his hands down his face, he tried to slow his breathing and calm the fuck down.

What was it about this guy that made him like this? He was like a teenager with his first crush, all bumbling words and sweaty palms.

"You're... I just... fuck." Aaron let his words trail off, instead looking up and meeting Mason's eyes, which sparkled with laughter.

"I love that I get you so flustered, and while this greeting is adorable, it's not what I was going for."

"Oh?"

Not saying anything further, Mason walked closer to him until they were pressed together and Aaron had to tip his head back to keep his gaze on Mason's face. Two large warm palms came up to hold his face, Aaron's lips parting on a sigh. Smirking, Mason lowered his head, joining their mouths together. Firm, a little bit wet, the kiss was everything Aaron didn't know he needed. All his tension evaporated as if it never was and he sank into the kiss and Mason's embrace, placing his hands overtop where Mason was holding his face so carefully.

"Hmm, that's better." Drawing back, Aaron met Mason's eyes, their bright and clear blue color like a cloudless winter day.

"What's happening here?" Aaron asked softly, his voice just above a whisper.

"I think you know, but if you're not ready to put it into words or even acknowledge it, that's okay. I'm patient."

Licking his lips, Aaron tried to swallow the lump in his throat but it didn't work. "I've never–"

"Shh." Mason silenced him by pressing his long

finger to his lips. "You don't need to say anything, I can see it all in your eyes."

Grunting, Aaron nodded, moving his hands to wrap them around Mason's neck and cling like a needy spider monkey. He had exactly zero fucks to give.

Chuckling, Mason wrapped his arms around his waist and picked him up, Aaron's feet dangling off the floor. Mason swayed side to side, tucking his face into Aaron's neck and humming with pleasure. "I love your smell."

"Are you saying I stink?" Aaron asked, incredulous.

"Of course not, dumpling! You smell like… home."

Melting on the inside and his cheeks blooming with color, yet again, Aaron responded the only way he could, he kissed his man.

CHAPTER 9

Mason's heart was thrumming in his chest, the feelings and emotions that this human male evoked in him nearly strangling him. In all his years, he'd never felt this way–about anyone. But he knew he couldn't give voice to his thoughts, he'd scare Aaron off, which was the last thing that he ever wanted to do.

Setting Aaron back onto his feet, Mason kept his hands on his waist, not wanting any distance between them. He couldn't keep his hands off his little human, nor did he want to.

"It's barely noon, what do you want to do today?" Mason asked, trying to force down the overwhelming urge to throw Aaron onto the floor and ravish him. Sex would come later, of that he had no doubt, but he wanted them to get to know each other better. Outside of sex.

"Hungry? I can make us some lunch. I haven't eaten yet today."

Frowning, he tugged Aaron into the kitchen. "Not eaten yet? That isn't good for you. Come, have a seat, I'll feed you."

Laughing, Aaron pulled his hand free. "Mason, it's okay. Seriously. I never eat breakfast."

"Nope. It's not okay. Sit." Pushing him down onto a bar stool, Mason pulled open the fridge door and sighed heavily. Once again, Aaron had little to no food in his house. "Aaron. What am I going to do with you? You need a keeper."

"You know, you're not the first person to tell me that. I get busy and I forget about food shopping and crap, so I just order in."

"So much takeout isn't good for you. I need you strong and healthy. Humans are so weak and fragile. A good diet will go a long way to keeping you around for a long time."

Blinking at him, Aaron's brow furrowed in confusion. "What?"

Sighing, knowing he said too much but unable to avoid the topic now, he continued, "I'm not immortal, but I'm very long lived. Undoubtably, I will outlive you, but I'd like for you to be around as long as possible."

"That's... sweet of you? I guess?" Aaron looked down at his lap, picking at his thumb nail.

"Never mind, it's not something you need to worry about right now. Just–let me take care of you, a little?"

Nodding, Aaron didn't say anything more and Mason would take the win where he could get it.

"Come on. We're going shopping." Letting the fridge door slam closed, Mason grabbed Aaron's hand and pulled him laughing toward the door. "I can't let you waste away to nothing, you need to keep your strength up."

Snagging his wallet, keys, and phone on the way, Aaron followed without protest. Following Mason out as they walked down the block to the market.

Arriving at the grocery store, Mason grabbed a cart and led the way straight to the meat department where he picked up bacon, steaks, hamburger, and chicken breasts. Aaron huffed, crossing his arms over his chest, but Mason just raised an eyebrow and continued onto the produce area.

Soon the cart was near to bursting with fresh vegetables, fruit, and more than a few bags of chips.

"Oh! Hang on, I almost forgot." Spotting the aisle he wanted, his grin burst free as he spotted to rows of sugary breakfast cereal. "Oh yes, there it is. My delicious beauties, come to papa." He snagged three boxes of Fruit Loops with marshmallows. On second thought, he added a fourth box, just to be on the safe side.

"Mason, my god. That stuff is hardly food. It's made of sugar and food coloring. How can you eat that?!"

"Easy, with milk and the biggest bowl I can hold comfortably. You don't understand. I was around when boxed cereal first came out and the box they came in had more flavor. There isn't much I love more in this world than Fruit Loops."

"Really? Nothing else?"

Chuckling, he snagged Aaron by the nape and hauled him closer for a quick, but sloppy kiss. "Well, there is something." Running his nose along Aaron's stubbly cheek until his mouth was next to his lover's ear, he purred, "Your ass comes to mind, I wouldn't mind snacking on that again later."

"Fucking hell, Mason. You know we're in public right? How am I supposed to walk around now when you say shit like that and make me hard?"

His responding laugh could only be described as evil, a fact that didn't disturb him in the least.

"Very carefully, dumpling, very carefully." Releasing Aaron, Mason turned the cart and headed to the registers.

After they paid, splitting the bill, much to Aaron's annoyance, Mason looked down at their collection of bags. He might have overdone it. They'd walked to the store and now they'd have to haul all this back to Aaron's apartment.

Snorting at their dilemma, Aaron got out his phone. "Hang on, dork, I'll call an Uber to come get us. You over shopped."

"I wouldn't have to over shop if you'd, ya know, *shop*, like, at all."

"Ooo, snarky. I like it."

Rolling his eyes, Mason crossed his arms over his chest and glared at the smaller man.

"Glare all you want; all it does is make my dick hard. Which will have to wait until I eat, because now I'm starving."

"Aaron!" Mason huffed, his grin breaking through. "You're delightful. Dammit. Where have you been all my life?"

"Being born, growing up, stuff like that. As you well know, you old ass."

It was the first time Aaron had directly referenced the life-long connection they had. Maybe they'd only met in the flesh on Christmas Eve, but they'd been in each other's lives for much longer than that. So, was this really so fast? Mason didn't know, but his heart swelled with joy and yes, love, for the man at his side.

"Old, maybe. But young enough to make you squeal, boy." Mason's smile was feral and more than a little dirty. Aaron returning his look in equal measure.

The Uber arrived just in time, because Mason was about to toss Aaron up against the wall and have him right here, right now. Lunch might have to wait.

AN HOUR LATER, Aaron was sprawled on his bed next to Mason, panting as they both tried to recover. Gasping, he spoke, "Has…anyone…ever…told you, you're a total power bottom? I mean, fuck. My dick almost hurts you rode me so hard."

"Maybe they have, but I'll never tell. I'm your power bottom, no one else's. Anyone who has came before you, doesn't matter to me. They all pale in comparison." Reaching down, Mason laced their fingers together, bringing their joined hands to his mouth where he placed a kiss to Aaron's knuckles.

"That's." Rolling to his side, facing Mason fully, Aaron continued, "I don't know what to say. You know about Gergory and what he meant to me. But this, whatever this is with you, is so much more intense. I'm not making much sense."

"Shh, you're making perfect sense. What we have will never replace what you had with him. Of course, it feels different. You're a different man now than you were then. And I'm not Gregory. He will always hold a place in your heart, I would never begrudge you that. But it doesn't lessen what we could have together. I know this is fast, scary fast, but I feel something for you. I don't ever want to let you go."

Leaning forward, Aaron molded their mouths together, nipping and sucking on Mason's tongue. His cock gave a half-hearted twitch, but he'd need more than five minutes to recover.

"Then don't. Don't let me go."

"Okay." Mason mumbled against Aaron's lips, not wanting to move enough even to speak. Pulling their bodies back into alignment, he decided he didn't need five minutes after all, and lunch could wait a little longer.

CHAPTER 10

Lunch was–finally–eaten and put away, Mason being surprisingly fussy about cleaning up after them.

"You don't even know, dumpling. I remember how things were before refrigeration." He shuddered. "It was less than pleasant, to say the least. You know ketchup was invented to cover the taste of spoiled meat? Be grateful for the preservatives and fridges. You don't want to know what life is like without it."

"Really? Ketchup was for more than on fries?" Aaron put the last dish away, before pouring a glass of water for each of them.

"Yeah, really. Crazy, huh?" Mason came up behind Aaron, caging him against the counter, tucking his face into the back of his neck, humming softly. "You smell like us."

Laughing, Aaron turned around to face him. "Are you saying I need a shower?" He nipped at Mason's chin, before kissing him lightly.

"Not at all. I love your scent. Makes me happy."

"That's so cheesy and sweet."

Snorting, Mason wrapped his huge arms around Aaron's waist and pulled him close. "You love it."

"Maybe." Smiling softly, Aaron allowed himself to feel his happiness in that moment. He didn't second guess it or analyze it. He wallowed in it. Basked. Clung the warm fuzzies close to his chest and let himself believe, even if for only this moment, that these soul-wrenching emotions were real and this was in fact–not a dream.

"I can feel your heart racing. Are you okay, dumpling?" Mason ran his palms up and down Aaron's back, calming him somewhat.

"Yeah. I'm good. This is all just… a lot."

"Is that–bad?" Mason's voice was soft and as hesitant as Aaron had ever heard it. Not that he'd heard it a lot. They'd only known each other less than a week. Was five days long enough to develop these kinds of bubbly, all consuming feelings? This was crazy!

"I'm not sure. I'm overwhelmed. Out of my depth. Whatever analogy you'd like to apply, that's me right now."

"Be still, dumpling. I'm not going anywhere. In all my years, I've seen more than you can ever imagine. I've seen people marry after only a few days and stay together their entire lives. I've also seen couples marry and grow apart, and everything in between. People grow and change. Just because it wasn't like this for you and Gregory doesn't mean that it's wrong now. What was right then, with him, isn't going to be the same as things are now, with me."

"What exactly is this? We keep dancing around it, but haven't labeled it."

Signing, Mason stepped back, releasing Aaron. He didn't like the space between them, he wanted to be plastered to every inch of Mason, always. Even during difficult discussions, maybe especially then.

"Does it have to be labeled? You're already spooked. Naming what we are will only make that worse."

Snapping his mouth closed, Aaron considered his words. Was that true? Would saying the words that they both felt pop the soap bubble surrounding them and smack them down into reality? With its harshness, bright light, and uncompromising truths?

Running both hands down his face, Aaron groaned, indecisive. "Everything with you is so intense. My head is spinning."

"What are you trying to say Aaron?"

Mason using his first name threw him momentarily. He'd gotten used to being called dumpling and he found he didn't like this serious side of Mason.

"Can I?" He paused, struggling to find the right words. "Would you mind if…?"

"Aaron, do you need some space?" Mason tucked his hands into the pockets of his jeans, his shoulders hunching with the movement.

"Y-yeah." Sighing heavily, Aaron turned pleading

eyes to Mason's face, expecting to see devastation or anger, but found nothing of the sort.

"And you thought I'd be upset?" Mason chuckled softly, before walking closer to him and clutching his shoulders, giving him a gentle shake.

"Well, yeah? You aren't?"

"Of course not! I know we don't know each other very well. Yet. But know this, dumpling, I. Am. Not. Going. Anywhere. Got it? If you need a day or two, that's more than fine and makes perfect sense."

"I've been alone for ten years, stuck in a rut of misery and grief. Then you come along all magical and wonderful and junk, and now I've done a total one-eighty. From one extreme to the other and my head is spinning and I don't know which way is up and I want you but I don't know *how* to have you and….and…"

"Aaron, it's okay. Seriously." Mason pressed their lips together softly. "Take what time you need; I only ask one thing."

"What's that?"

"Text me? Keep in touch, at least once a day or so, just so I know that you're okay."

Heart melting, Aaron nodded. "I can do that, of course."

"Good. Now give me a kiss and you can walk me out."

Grinning up at Mason and feeling lighter than he could ever remember being, Aaron obliged him.

❄

THE NEXT DAY, Aaron returned home from going for a run and unlocked his apartment and walked in. It had been twenty-four-ish hours since he'd seen Mason, but it felt much longer. He was changed in a fundamental way. He didn't have the words to express how he felt. Unburdened maybe? He was sure he was going to float away any second.

Dropping his keys on the table near the door, he kicked off his shoes, and headed directly to the shower. He was sweaty, despite running in the cold, and catching another whiff of himself, he grimaced.

Stripping down, he started the shower and looked at himself in the mirror while he waited for the water to heat. The perpetual dark circles under his eyes were nearly gone; also missing was the dull sheen to his eyes. Now they were clear and bright, full of a look he hadn't seen on himself in too long. It was as foreign as it was welcome.

"It's okay to feel good. It's okay to be happy. You're allowed to find love again. You're allowed to hope." He spoke to himself, hoping his affirmations stuck.

Stepping into his shower, he let the hot water rain down upon him and wash away the sticky sweat that clung to his skin. He heaved a sigh of bliss, groaning as his tight muscles relaxed. Steam billowed around him in a dense cloud, he breathed deep and reached for the body wash. Pumping some into his hands, he began to wash, his mind wandering, as ever, back to Mason.

Smoothing his hands down his chest, he cupped

his cock and balls, rolling his sack with one hand while tugging himself to full hardness with the other. His mind went directly to memories of Mason in his bed. Of his moans and cries of pleasure, to the hot clench of his ass around his cock.

"Ugh…" He moaned to himself, his hand gripping harder and moving faster, twisting slightly at the head. He let go of his balls with his left hand and instead reached behind himself, sliding his slippery fingers over his hole. Not pushing inside, instead circling and teasing. He felt empty, hollowed out.

The thought stopped him in his tracks. Fuck.

He wanted Mason.

Jerking off and fingering himself in the shower was a pathetic replacement for the real thing. For what, and who, he really wanted. His magical snowman, with his gleaming glacier blue eyes and strong arms. Aaron needed his deep voice rumbling in his ear, calling him dumpling and worshiping every inch of his skin.

Resolute, Aaron rinsed quickly, not even bothering to wash his hair.

Was this insane? Yes. Did he care? Not a fuckin' bit.

CHAPTER 11

Mason jerked awake at the sound of someone pounding on his door.

Boom. Boom. Boom. A pause. *Boom. Boom. Boom.*

"Fuck! I'm coming. Jesus, lay the hell off." He was grumpy, his temper on a hair trigger. Aaron hadn't kept his promise, he hadn't texted or called. Radio fuckin silence and he was pissed off. Whoever was at his door better have a good reason or they were going to be a popsicle.

Dressed only in boxer briefs, Mason stormed to the door and jerked it open. Shock freezing him in place when he saw who was standing there.

"Aaron?"

"Nope." Red faced and with a crazy look in his eyes, Aaron braced both hands on the door frame and stared Mason down.

"What?"

"Not Aaron."

"Erm… I'm confused." Mason scratched his left pec, suddenly nervous and unsure of himself. What was happening here?

"Don't call me Aaron." His lover growled, smacking his hands against the wood of the frame.

"Well, that is your name. What else am I supposed to call you?" His brain misfired, hope beginning to grow as the pieces began to fall together.

"Yours. You're supposed to call me yours. Now. Tomorrow. And every day after that."

Grinning, Mason curled a fist in Aaron t-shirt and jerked him forward so the smaller man stumbled into him, flattening his hands against Mason's bare chest.

"Is that so, dumpling?" Ducking his head, Mason ran his nose along the skin of Aaron's throat, inhaling deeply. He'd never tire of his scent.

"Yes. I don't need any more space."

As if to prove his point, Aaron wrapped his arms around Mason's waist and shuffled them backward into the apartment. He kicked the door closed behind them, even while he licked a path from Mason's collarbone to his ear, before sucking the lobe into his mouth.

Mason shuddered, his cock hardening, stretching the fabric of his boxer briefs.

"No more space huh? I'm feeling a little dumb right now. All my blood has travelled south and my big brain is suffering for it. Spell it out for me, dumpling."

Aaron moved back just enough to hold Mason's face with both hands, running his thumbs gently along his cheekbones. Their eyes met, Mason's hopeful and Aaron's unflinching. "I love you."

A wide grin broke free, pulling each side of Mason's mouth up. "That didn't take nearly as long as I expected."

Sputtering Aaron gaped up at him. "What?"

"I've loved you since you kissed me in the park and brought me back to life. I was just waiting for you to catch up. You got there quicker than I anticipated. Good job, dumpling."

"You're impossible!"

Aaron's tone and sparkling eyes didn't match his tone. Sliding his hands up the small of Aaron's back, shoving up Aaron's shirt impatiently, he sought out his skin. His palms met warm flesh and he groaned. His traced the bumps in Aaron's spine, up and then back down, loving the shiver he got in response.

"Impossibly in love. It's fast, it's intense, more than a little crazy. But it's us."

"I still feel like I'm in a Hallmark movie, but I'm done being scared."

Chuckling, Mason tugged Aaron's shirt over his head, tossing it aside and going right for the snap of his jeans. "Hallmark, dumpling? Nah, we're NC17."

Tipping his head back, Aaron roared with laughter. Mason took advantage and bit gently over his exposed Adam's apple. "X rated…"

"You're damn right." He stripped his lover bare

and carried him to his bedroom, knowing in his heart
he wouldn't be living here much longer. He couldn't
wait to make a home with Aaron. To care for him,
treasure him, and love him for as long as he lived.

72

EPILOGUE

Two Years Later, Christmas Eve . . .

Aaron curled his gloved fingers around Mason's as they walked home from seeing Aaron's family. It was almost midnight, snow was falling gently, and all around them lights sparkled against the blanket of snow covering their little town.

"This reminds me so much of the night we met." Aaron said, tipping his head back to catch a snowflake on his tongue. Giggling as Mason waved his hand and a small flurry puffed onto his face. "Hey!" He sputtered, wiped the snow off his cheeks.

"Just wanted to make sure you got one."

Bumping his shoulder into his husband's, he altered their course to go through the park. "Smart ass."

"Maybe, but you love my ass." Winking, Mason

pulled his hand from Aaron's and draped his arm over his shoulder.

"Too true. Along with the rest of you."

"What's not to love?" Mason leaned down, capturing Aaron's chilly lips in a soft kiss, which quickly deepened. Their tongues tangled and Aaron's hands ended up in Mason's hair, tugging him ever closer.

Laughing against his husband's mouth, joy like he never imagined he'd feel burst through him.

"Maybe when you drink too much and bury our bed under a foot of snow in your sleep?"

Scoffing, Mason pulled back, guiding them toward their home. "That was *one* time! You're never going to let me live that down, are you?"

Smirking up at Mason, Aaron replied, "Nope."

"A lifetime of you busting my balls?"

"Would you want it any other way?" Aaron asked as they passed the gazebo and the yearly ice sculpture display, minus a snowman with a cheeky grin. His heart warming at the memory, forever grateful that he'd taken this path that night, that he'd believed in magic again and took a chance on a snowman's kiss.

"Never."

Sometimes, just sometimes, wishes do come true.

The End

OTHER BOOKS BY J.B. HAVENS

<u>ROMANCE:</u>

Snowman Wishes

ANTELOPE ROCK SERIES
CO-AUTHORED WITH SAMANTHA A. COLE
Wannabe in Wyoming
Wistful in Wyoming

<u>MILITARY SUSPENSE:</u>

STEEL CORPS SERIES
Core of Steel

Hardened by Steel

Forged by Steel

Bound by Steel

Solid Steel

STEEL CORPS/TRIDENT SECURITY CROSSOVERS WITH SAMANTHA A. COLE

No Way in Hell

<u>SCI-FI HORROR:</u>

ABOUT J.B. HAVENS

J.B. Havens lives in rural Pennsylvania, and is a wife and mother of three, a boy and twin girls. She has a love for a good cheesesteak and anything that involves coffee or chocolate. When she's not caring for her family, she is busy researching and writing her next novel.

Find JB on her website where you can find character bios and even a short story or two. She loves to hear from readers, so reach out and tell her what you think!

Connect with J.B.

Facebook
Haven's Haven Facebook Group
Twitter